Dear Parents,

Welcome to the Scholastic Reader series. We have taken over 80 years of experience with teachers, parents, and children and put it into a program that is designed to match your child's interests and skills.

Level 1—Short sentences and stories made up of words kids can sound out using their phonics skills and words that are important to remember.

Level 2—Longer sentences and stories with words kids need to know and new "big" words that they will want to know.

Level 3—From sentences to paragraphs to longer stories, these books have large "chunks" of texts and are made up of a rich vocabulary.

Level 4—First chapter books with more words and fewer pictures.

It is important that children learn to read well enough to succeed in school and beyond. Here are ideas for reading this book with your child:

- Look at the book together. Encourage your child to read the title and make a prediction about the story.
- Read the book together. Encourage your child to sound out words when appropriate. When your child struggles, you can help by providing the word.
- Encourage your child to retell the story. This is a great way to check for comprehension.
- Have your child take the fluency test on the last page to check progress.

Scholastic Readers are designed to support your child's efforts to learn how to read at every age and every stage. Enjoy helping your child learn to read and love to read.

— **Francie Alexander**
Chief Education Officer
Scholastic Education

For Ryan Halloran, the newest reader in the family
— M.P.

To Kellyn and Kye
— D.R.

Text copyright © 1999 by Mary Packard.
Illustrations copyright © 1999 by Dana Regan.
Fluency activities copyright © 2003 Scholastic Inc.

All rights reserved. Published by Scholastic Inc.
SCHOLASTIC, CARTWHEEL BOOKS, and associated logos are trademarks
and/or registered trademarks of Scholastic Inc.

ISBN 0-439-59425-1

Library of Congress Cataloging-in-Publication Data is available.

16 15 14 13 12 11 10   14 15/0

Printed in the U.S.A. 40

First printing, October 1999

FALL LEAVES

by Mary Packard
Illustrated by Dana Regan

Scholastic Reader — Level 1

SCHOLASTIC INC.

New York   Toronto   London   Auckland   Sydney
Mexico City   New Delhi   Hong Kong   Buenos Aires

Did someone paint
the leaves I see?

They seem to shout,
"Hey, look at me!"

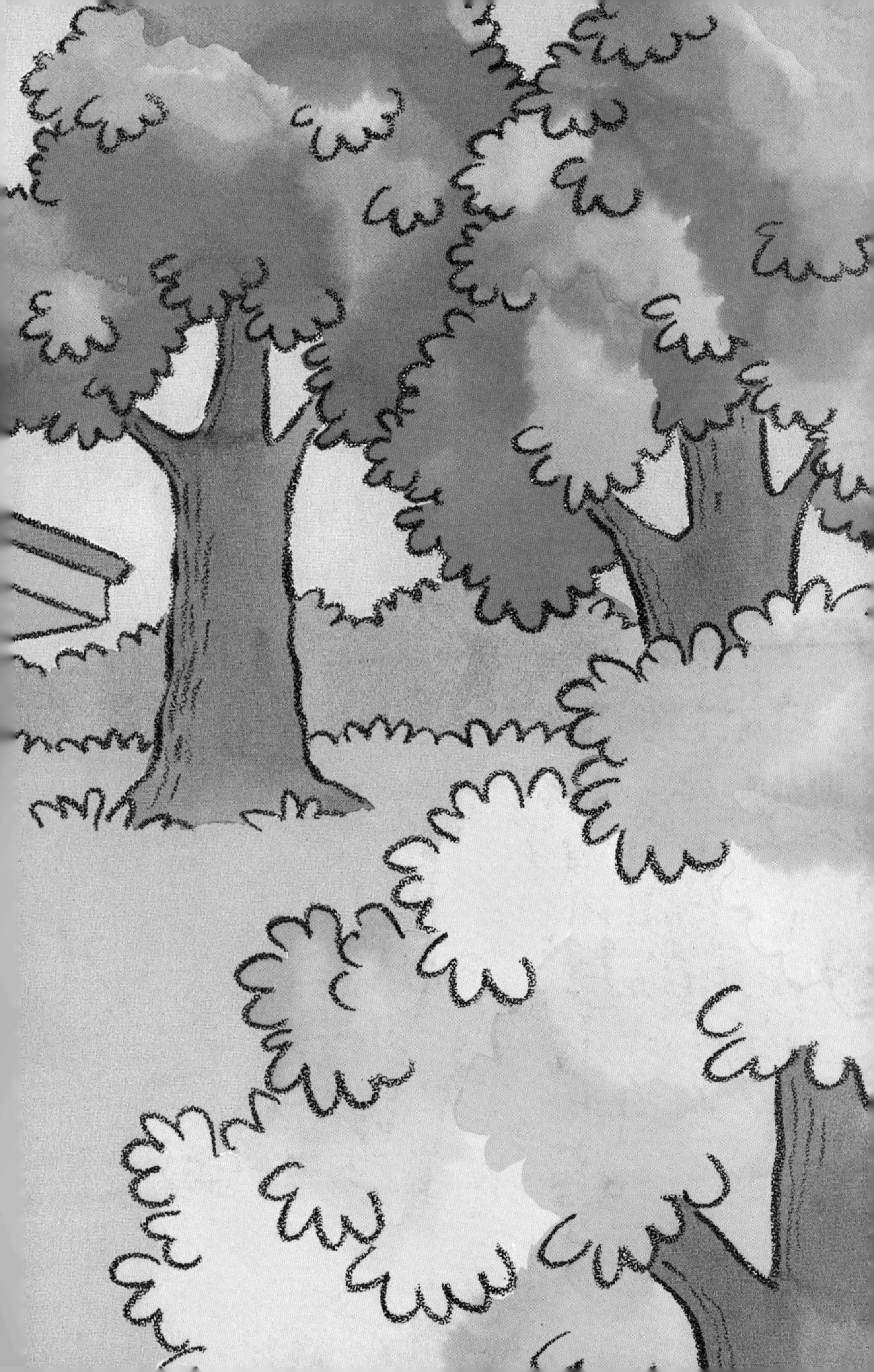

Leaves of gold and leaves of red
tell of fun-filled days ahead.

Fun for chipmunks.

Fun for squirrels.

Fun for boys and fun for girls!

Fun to bat them in the air.

Fun to chase them
here and there.

Small leaves, thin leaves, fat and round

are fun to hunt for
on the ground.

Good for making leafy shapes
of slinky snakes and silly apes.

Good for crunching under feet
on the way to trick or treat.

Good for raking in big piles.

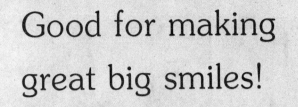

Good for making great big smiles!

Hide and Seek

There are five squirrels hidden in this picture.
Can you find them?

F is for Fall

Point to the pictures whose names begin with the letter **f**.

Rhyme Time

Point to the picture that rhymes with the word
at the beginning of each row.

air

me

fat

ape

fall

Animal Match-Up

Match each animal with the sentence that describes it.

I am brown with a bushy tail.

I am small and have a white stripe.

I have long whiskers.

I like to wag my tail.

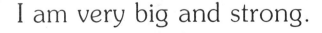

I get around without any feet.

I am very big and strong.

Word Search

The words on the left are in the puzzle below.
Can you find them?

fall   fun

days   look

E F U N B M
D A Y S Y E
J L B W S G
R L O O K X

Fall Fun

Which of these fall activities is your favorite?
Tell what makes it fun.

ANSWERS

Hide and Seek

F is for Fall

Rhyme Time

air
me
fat
ape
fall

Animal Match Up

I am brown with a bushy tail.

I am small and have a white stripe.

I have long whiskers.

I like to wag my tail.

I get around without any feet.

I am very big and strong.

Word Search

```
E  F  U  N  B  M
D  A  Y  S  Y  E
J  L  B  W  S  G
R  L  O  O  K  X
```

Fall Fun

Answers will vary.

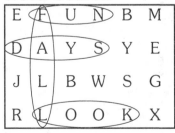